Kidnapped

Robert Louis Stevenson

Adapted by Margaret McAllister

Illustrated by Martin Cottam

OXFORD
UNIVERSITY PRESS

About the Author

ROBERT LOUIS STEVENSON
1850 – 1894

Robert Louis Balfour Stevenson was born in Edinburgh in 1850. As a child he was often ill with lung problems and had to stay in bed, where he loved hearing and making up stories. His father's work as an engineer took him all over Scotland, and Stevenson sometimes travelled with him.

Stevenson studied law, but he wanted to travel and be a writer. His health became so bad that he had to leave the Scottish climate and live in Europe, where he began to write articles and books about his journeys.

He wrote his adventure story, *Treasure Island,* in 1883 and *Kidnapped* in 1886. He used his memories of his travels around Scotland and his love of sea journeys to write *Kidnapped*.

Stevenson and his wife, Frances, settled at last in the Pacific Island of Samoa. He died suddenly on 3 December 1894, aged 44.

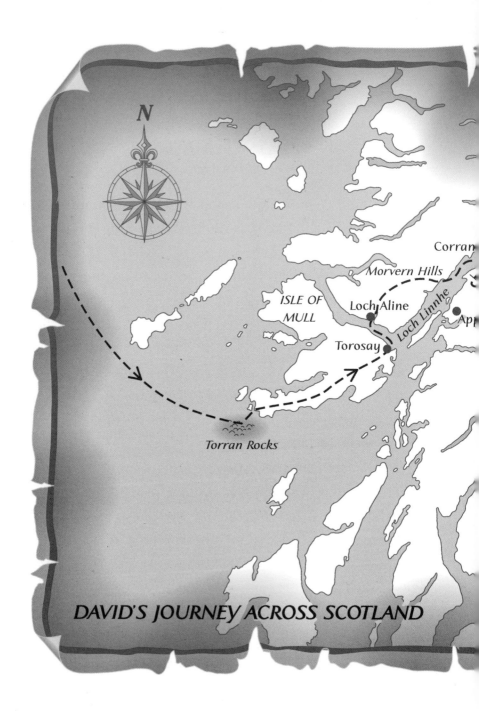

N

Corran

Morvern Hills

ISLE OF
MULL

Loch Aline

Loch Linnhe

Ap

Torosay

Torran Rocks

DAVID'S JOURNEY ACROSS SCOTLAND

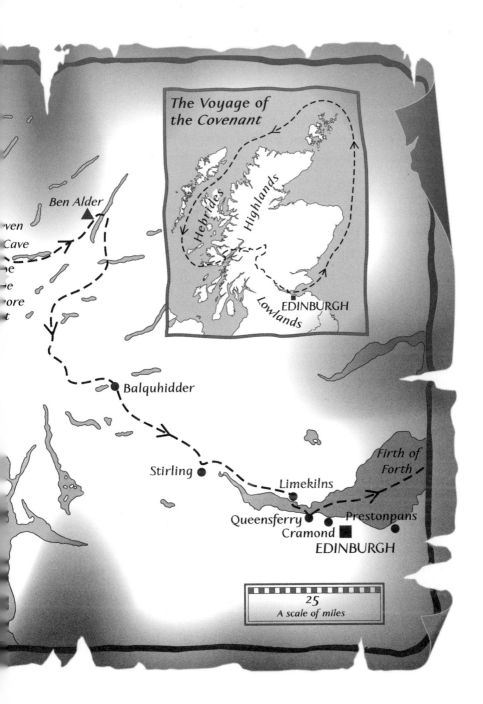

Ben Alder

Cave

ore

The Voyage of
the Covenant

Hebrides

Highlands

EDINBURGH

Lowlands

Balquhidder

Firth of
Forth

Stirling

Limekilns

Queensferry   Prestonpans

Cramond

EDINBURGH

25
A scale of miles

Background

To enjoy this book, it helps if you understand a little about what was happening in Scotland when this story was set.

King George II ruled over England and Scotland, but many people, especially in Scotland, believed that the rightful king of England and Scotland was James Stuart. This was because he descended from the Stuart kings. When George II was made king, James was in exile in Europe.

Jacobites and Whigs

King George's supporters were called Whigs and James's supporters were called Jacobites. Most Whigs were Protestant Lowlanders and most Jacobites were Catholic Highlanders.

Campbells

The Campbell family were Whigs. King George gave them a lot of power in Scotland and the Jacobites hated them.

Battle of Culloden 1746

In 1745 James's son, Bonnie Prince Charlie, came to Scotland to lead a Jacobite army against the English. This was known as the 1745 Rebellion. The Jacobites suffered a terrible defeat at the Battle of Culloden in 1746, and George II remained king. From then on, the English leaders did everything they could to make the Jacobites suffer. Many Jacobite chiefs escaped to France.

Kidnapped

Kidnapped is set in 1751. At this time, the Jacobites were still suffering after the Battle of Culloden. This story is based on real events that occurred in 1751 but the main characters in the story are not real.

CHAPTER I

Leaving Home

On a morning in June 1751, I locked the door of my father's house for the last time. I was sixteen years old. Now that my parents were dead I had, as far as I knew, no family at all. I was leaving to make my own way in the world.

One good friend – our minister, Mr Campbell – was waiting for me at the gate. 'I will start you on your journey, David,' he said, as we walked away from the house. 'I have a letter here for you, which should be useful. Your father wrote it when he was dying, and you are to take it to the House of Shaws at Cramond, near Edinburgh.'

I had never heard of the House of Shaws, and said so. I was just David Balfour, the son of a poor country schoolmaster in Essendean, a Scottish village in the lowlands. As Mr Campbell put the letter into my hand I read the address – 'Ebenezer Balfour of Shaws'. So it seemed that I was connected to a grand family – Balfour of the House of Shaws sounded impressive! My future might be brighter than I had imagined.

'It will only be two days' walk to get there,' said Mr

Campbell, 'and if you are not welcomed, turn round, walk the two days back and come to me.'

He reminded me, as I knew he would, that I must always say my prayers, read my Bible, and work hard. Then he tugged a small parcel from his pocket.

'Here is the money from the sale of your father's books and furniture,' he said, 'and a gift from Mrs Campbell and myself.' Then he said a prayer with me, hugged me, and, close to tears, hurried away.

The parting moved him more than it did me. I was young, full of hope, and looking forward to meeting my grand relations.

Opening the parcel, I found a Bible, money, and a recipe for a medicine that was meant to cure everything from gout to sprained ankles. It made me laugh, but the Campbells' kindness touched me. With my small bundle of belongings over my shoulder, I crossed the ford and, looking back once more at the only home I had ever known, I set off.

On the second day of my journey I reached a hill-top and looked down at Edinburgh, with its smoking chimneys. Ships lay anchored in the harbour. I had heard of the Firth of Forth[1] before, but never seen it.

---

[1] A firth is a river-mouth. The Firth of Forth is where the river Forth flows into the sea near Edinburgh.

By asking directions I found my way to the village of
Cramond, and the next step was to find the House of
Shaws where Ebenezer Balfour lived. This was much
more difficult. Everyone I asked looked warily at me. A
carter warned me to avoid the place. Nobody would even
discuss Ebenezer Balfour.

I was having doubts about my supposedly fine
relations. I could have gone straight back to Mr and Mrs

Campbell, but I felt I had to finish what I had started. Finally, at sunset, I saw a stout, dark woman coming towards me, and I asked her the way to the House of Shaws. She turned, trudged uphill, and pointed into a valley.

The valley was green and pleasant, and spoiled only by an almost derelict mansion. It must have been grand once, but now it was crumbling away. It had no path, no garden, and no chimney smoke. It looked deserted.

'That?' I cried.

'House of Shaws!' she screeched. 'Blood built it, and blood shall bring it down! Black be its fall! For the twelve hundredth and nineteenth time, Jennet Clouston curses it!' Then she turned and ran.

I sat down and looked at this miserable house. Eventually, I saw a wisp of chimney smoke. Somebody must have come home. I walked down towards it, but it looked worse at every step. One wing had never been finished, and there were empty windows where bats flew in and out. My father's house had been small and poor, but it had always looked welcoming.

I knocked at the door wondering what sort of person would open it, but nobody did, though I thought I could hear someone coughing inside. Angry that somebody was deliberately ignoring me, I knocked harder, and shouted the name of Mr Balfour.

A window opened above me. Looking down was a man wearing a nightcap, and pointing a blunderbuss[2] at me.

'I have a letter for Mr Ebenezer Balfour of the House of Shaws,' I called up.

'Leave it, and go!' he ordered.

'Certainly not!' I said. 'It is a letter to introduce myself. I am David Balfour.'

He jerked with surprise. Then he muttered, 'Your father would never send you here if he was alive. He must be dead, then. Well, I'll let you in.' He disappeared from the window.

---

[2] A hand-gun.

My Uncle

With much rattling of chains and bolts the door was opened. It was locked again the moment I was inside, and I stood in the barest room I had ever seen. There was a table with a bowl of porridge and a mug of beer, and plain chests and cupboards, all locked. Nothing else. I saw this by firelight, for there were no candles.

I could see the man clearly now. He was pale and shrivelled, and wore a ragged nightgown. He watched

me without looking me in the eyes, which made me uneasy.

'If you're hungry, eat that,' he said, nodding towards the porridge. I protested that it was his own supper, but he said he only wanted a drink. He asked for the letter.

'It's for Mr Balfour,' I said.

'Who d'you think I am?' he growled. 'You're Alexander Balfour's son, aren't you? I'm your Uncle Ebenezer.'

So this was my only living relation! He may have been my father's brother, but he looked as old and uninviting as the house. Handing over the letter, I found I no longer had an appetite for porridge, nor anything else.

'I expect you want me to help you,' he grumbled.

'I ask no favours,' I answered. I had my pride. My uncle gobbled down the porridge I had refused, glancing up suspiciously.

'Did your father speak of me?' he asked.

'Never,' I said, and he seemed relieved to hear it. Then he clapped me on the shoulder and offered me a room to sleep in.

With neither lamp nor candle he led me up to a chamber. I asked for a light, but he said that he feared lights in the house and that the full moon was light enough. He left me, and locked the door.

It was a damp, dark room and cold even on this

summer night. When morning came I saw it was also filthy, with broken windows. The furnishings had been nibbled by mice and cobwebbed by spiders. I banged on the door and shouted until my uncle let me out, and we had a small breakfast of more porridge.

'I'll do something to help you,' he muttered. 'I'll get you into the law, or maybe the army. But mind, no talking about me to your friends in Essendean, or you'll be out of my house.'

It was time to assert myself. 'I'll go anyway, if you

speak like that,' I said. Suddenly he changed his attitude and said that families must be loyal to each other. Wondering how he would respond, I told him of the woman, Jennet Clouston, who had screamed a curse at the house.

'The old witch!' he cried. 'It's her own fault I had her turned out of her house! I'm going to the magistrate about her!' He reached for his hat. 'I must lock you out while I am gone,' he said.

'Lock me out?' I cried. 'Then I'll never come back! You hate having me here, you treat me like a thief! Will you help me, or will I go back to Essendean?'

At that, he seemed to change his mind. 'No, no!' he said. 'Stay here. We'll agree fine.'

I wasn't at all convinced by his sudden attempt to be reasonable, but I agreed to stay. He was, after all, the only relation I had.

My uncle stayed home, and I avoided him. Our midday meal was porridge again, eaten in silence. In the afternoon I found some books to pass the lonely time, and discovered something that puzzled me.

Ebenezer had inherited the family House of Shaws, so he must have been the elder brother. But I found a book with these words inside – 'to my brother Ebenezer on his fifth birthday.' My father must have been less than four years old when he wrote that!

Later I mentioned to Uncle Ebenezer that my father must have been quick to learn.

'No,' he said. 'I could read as soon as he could.'

'Oh, were you twins?' I asked.

He jumped up, grabbed my jacket, and demanded, 'What do you mean?' Then he calmed down and pretended that it upset him to speak of my father, but I watched him as suspiciously as he watched me.

When we finished our meal – porridge again – he said, 'Davie, I have put some money aside for you.' He paused as if the subject pained him. 'All of forty pounds. But you must stand at the door while I get it.'

I could tell he was trying some sort of trick, and it amused me that he thought I could be fooled so easily. I waited outside the door while he fetched the money. A storm was gathering. There were few stars, and the air felt heavy with thunder. My uncle called me in at last, counted the coins slowly and reluctantly into my hand, and said, 'Now, Davie, we need to look at some papers concerning the house. Will you fetch them? Go up the spiral stair to the wee room right at the top. You'll find the documents in a chest.'

As the house was five storeys high and, as my uncle would not allow lights, I climbed the stairs in blackness, feeling my way with one hand on the wall. As I climbed higher, the thunderstorm broke. The air felt cooler – then a flash of lightning showed me where I was. Fear left me powerless.

It was as if I stood on scaffolding. The walls were crumbling, the steps were uneven. I stood two paces away from a sheer drop. This was what my uncle planned for me – to plunge to my death.

Anger gave me courage. I felt my way down the stairs. A flash of lightning showed my uncle standing outside in

the storm, listening until a crash of thunder sent him scurrying to the kitchen. He poured a strong drink and, shuddering, gulped it down. I stepped up behind him and clapped him on the shoulder. With a cry of horror, he collapsed. He lay so long I feared he was dead, but his eyelids fluttered open. He looked at me in terror.

'Are you still alive?' he sobbed. I felt sorry for his terror and weakness, but I was still angry as he begged me to let him go to bed. I demanded an explanation.

'In the morning,' he promised, and I agreed. I felt I had the better of him now, and had nothing to fear. So I locked him in his bedroom, made up a great blazing fire in the hearth, and settled down to sleep beside it.

CHAPTER 3

The Covenant

In the morning I unlocked the room, sure that I had got the better of him. Before I could demand an explanation there was a knock at the door, and the oddest looking lad stood shivering on the doorstep.

He was only a boy but he was dressed as a sailor, and danced hornpipe[3] steps, presumably to warm himself. He looked as if he was about to laugh or cry.

'Got a letter,' he said, grinning. 'From old Heasy-Oasy to Mr Belflower.' (He meant 'Balfour'.) 'I'm starving hungry.'

I sat him at the table where he crammed porridge into his mouth, all the time winking and grimacing at me in a way that I suppose was meant to be manly. My uncle read the letter and handed it to me –

Hawes Inn
Queensferry

Sir, my ship is about to sail. Any business between us must be settled at once.

Yours,
Elias Hoseason

'Captain Hoseason,' said my uncle, 'is the captain of a trading ship, the *Covenant*. She lies at anchor at Queensferry, and I must see him before she sails. We'll go

---

[3] A sailor's dance.

together. While we're at Queensferry we can visit Mr Rankeillor, the family lawyer. He's a respectable old man. He knew your father.'

I still did not trust him, but I was eager to talk to Mr Rankeillor, so we all set out for Queensferry. The boy, I discovered, was the *Covenant's* cabin boy, Ransome. He tried to impress me by showing how grown-up he was, but to him, 'grown-up' meant swearing and boasting of all the wicked deeds he claimed to have done. He described Captain Hoseason ('Heasy-Oasy' to him,) as a brutal man, and admired him for it. The mate,[4] Mr Shuan, was even worse, and Ransome had bruises to show for it. The poor boy was proud of them.

He loved to exaggerate. He even told me that the *Covenant* carried innocent people who had been kidnapped, and were sold into slavery in tobacco plantations. By the time we had reached the small town of Queensferry, near Edinburgh, I had heard as much as I could bear. The *Covenant* lay at anchor in the Firth of Forth and, although I pitied those who sailed in her, I longed to see her. I had never been near a ship before.

My uncle took me to an inn where a tall, dark man sat at a table. This was Captain Hoseason, who looked as calm and solemn as a judge. The room was too hot, and my first glimpse of the harbour made me yearn to see

---

[4] A ship's officer.

more. I still did not completely trust my uncle, but I was so keen to get out and explore that I left him with the captain.

Walking on the beach, I watched the sailors preparing the *Covenant*. Presently, I met Ransome again. Following his urgent hints I took him to a tavern and bought ale for us both, though he was wheedling for something stronger. The landlord was watching me.

'Were you with Mr Ebenezer?' he asked.

I said I was, adding that Ebenezer Balfour seemed unpopular.

'Aye,' he said, 'ever since the old rumour about him and his brother.'

'What rumour?' I asked.

'Oh, years ago, when Alexander left the House of Shaws,' he said. 'People said Ebenezer had killed him to get the house. Alexander was the elder son.'

The elder son. I had guessed as much, but now I knew it to be true. The house had rightfully been my father's, and should have passed to me. I was the heir to a fortune – if any of it was left.

Leaving the tavern, I met Captain Hoseason and my uncle. The Captain was so pleasant and courteous that I was sure Ransome, the cabin boy, had been unfair to describe him as a brute.

'I hope you'll come on the ship, before she sails,' he said. 'I'd like you to see over her.'

'We must see Mr Rankeillor,' I said, but I wanted with all my heart to see the ship.

'The ship's boat can take you to the pier, near his house,' he said. Then he drew me aside and whispered,

'I need to speak to you. You can't trust your uncle.'

My mind was made up. The small ship's boat took us as far as the *Covenant*, where I was lifted aboard and the captain showed me over the gently rocking deck.

'But where is my uncle?' I asked.

Then I saw him. The ship's boat was returning to shore, with Ebenezer in it, leaving me on board a slave ship. As I shouted after him he turned and I was amazed to see a terrible look of fear and cruelty. Then something that felt like a thunderbolt struck me, and I lost consciousness.

I came round in darkness. My hands and feet were tied and I lay in pain, surrounded by the roaring of waters and shouting of sailors. The ship lurched. Pain and nausea were made worse by my anger. I raged against my uncle's treachery and my own stupidity at being tricked, just because I wanted to see the ship.

I was too ill to eat or drink and it must have been days before a sailor brought in a lantern and tried to help me. He was a small man with green eyes and fair hair. He felt my pulse, cleaned the wound on my head, and offered me food. I still could not eat, so he brought me brandy and water instead.

In spite of his kindness, I became worse. I felt dizzy, I

ached and burned and knew I was feverish. At last the sailor returned, bringing the captain.

'We must move him to the forecastle,'[5] said the sailor.

'He stays here, Mr Riach,' said the captain.

---

[5] A place in the bow (front part of the ship), where the crew sleep. Forecastle is pronounced 'foaksle'.

'*You* may have been paid to do a murder,' said Mr Riach, 'but I was not.'

'Stop that talk!' ordered the captain. 'You may be a second officer on this ship, but you wouldn't talk like this if you hadn't been drinking. If you think the lad will die, move him to where you like.'

Within five minutes I was moved to the forecastle, where the sailors had their quarters. They were rough men, used to hard lives and cruelties and quick to fight, but they treated me well enough.

I learned much of the ship and its crew. The ship had two mates – Riach, the one who had befriended me, and Shuan. Both drank heavily. Riach was in a better mood drunk than sober, and Shuan was the opposite. Ransome waited on the captain and the mates in their quarters in the roundhouse.[6] When I saw Ransome bruised and crying, I knew Shuan had been drinking and taking out his rage on the boy. Poor Ransome! He had never known anything but cruelty.

I learned too, what Uncle Ebenezer had arranged. The ship was sailing to the Carolinas.[7] There I would be sold as a slave, to work on tobacco plantations for the rest of my life.

About nine o'clock one night, a whisper began to go round the forecastle. 'Shuan has done for him,' said the sailors.

Nobody asked who they meant, and nobody needed to. Captain Hoseason opened the scuttle[8] that led into the forecastle, climbed down the ladder, and walked straight to me.

'David, we need you to serve in the roundhouse,' he said, and spoke very kindly. 'We need you to change

---

[6] A raised cabin in the stern (back of a ship), for officers.

[7] North and South Carolina, in America, were well known for using slave labour on the cotton and tobacco plantations.

[8] A small opening, like a trapdoor.

places with Ransome. Run away aft!'[9]

As he spoke, two sailors went past the scuttle and I could see that they carried Ransome in their arms. At that moment the ship lurched, the lantern swung, and the light fell on the boy's face, which was white in death and fixed with an appalling leer. I stood horrified.

'Run aft!' ordered the captain. As the ship swayed, I staggered to the officers' quarters in the roundhouse.

The roundhouse was higher than the decks, with a table and chairs, sleeping berths[10] and storage lockers. The firearms[11] were kept here, and much of the food and drink. Mr Shuan sat silently at the table, with a brandy bottle in front of him. Hoseason joined him, then Riach, but nobody spoke until Shuan reached for the bottle. Riach snatched it from him.

'You've murdered the boy!' shouted the captain. Shuan looked vaguely round as if he was trying to understand what he had done. The captain put him to bed, and muttered with Mr Riach about how they would cover up the story.

That was the beginning of my work in the roundhouse, which was mostly serving meals and

---

[9] Towards the stern, the back of the ship.

[10] Sleeping places.

[11] Guns.

keeping the officers supplied with drink. Strong drink was always wanted, and I was often roused from sleep to serve them. They did not treat me as cruelly as they had treated Ransome. They allowed me a full share of the food. I believe they felt guilty about Ransome's death and were trying to compensate for it, but in my heart I raged at the way I had been cheated. I was serving three men whom I despised, and who intended to sell me into slavery.

CHAPTER 4

The Highlander

Soon after the murder came a night of fog and foul weather. Suddenly, with a crash, the ship lurched horribly. In the fog we had hit another boat so violently that she split in two and sank. One man survived by clinging to the bowsprit,[12] and the captain brought him into the roundhouse.

He looked amazingly calm. He was small, with a pleasant expression on a sunburnt, pockmarked face, and his eyes had a brightness that both attracted and alarmed me. He wore a feathered hat and a fine blue coat with lace and silver buttons. On the table he laid a pair of silver-mounted pistols, and I saw that he wore a sword. Here, I thought, was a man I would rather have as a friend than an enemy.

'Good friends of mine have gone down today,' he said.

'Friends in French coats, like yours?' asked Hoseason.

The stranger looked up warily. 'Are you of the honest party?' he asked.

This question worried me. Like most Lowland Scots, my religion was Protestant and I was loyal to King

---

[12] A long post or mast, extending over the front of a ship.

George. I was, in other words, a Whig. When the
stranger said, 'the honest party', he meant he was a
Jacobite. Jacobites were mostly Catholic Highlanders,
and said that James Stuart was the rightful King of

Scotland. They wanted to throw out the ruling King George. A few years back in 1745 the Jacobites, led by Bonnie Prince Charlie, had rebelled against King George, but had been soundly defeated in the Battle of Culloden. Many had escaped to France. As a Lowlander, my minister Mr Campbell had taught me to have nothing to do with Jacobites.

'I was going to France,' said the stranger to Hoseason. 'I'll pay you well to take me there.'

'Not France,' said the captain. 'Maybe I could take you back to Scotland?' He sent me to bring supper. When I returned, the Jacobite had taken a money-belt from his waist and placed coins on the table. Hoseason looked at the belt.

'For half of all you have, I'll help you,' said the captain.

'None of it's mine,' said the man. 'It is for my clan[13] chief in France. I only spend money on myself to make sure that the rest reaches him. Sixty guineas if you take me safely to Loch Linnhe, where I can find a ship to France.'

The captain argued, but he agreed at last. I knew that trustworthy Jacobites collected money from their clans in Scotland to take to the exiled chiefs in France, but I had never expected to meet one of them. The redcoats[14] hunted them down.

---

[13] A group of families, all related to each other, led by a clan chief.
[14] English soldiers in red uniforms.

The captain left us. The stranger asked for a drink but the bottle was empty, so I went to ask for the key to the whisky cupboard. Through the fog on deck I saw Hoseason, Shuan and Riach, and heard lowered voices.

'Keep him in the roundhouse,' Hoseason was saying. 'He hasn't room to use a sword in there, and it's three against one.'

Anger seized me. They were planning to murder a brave man who meant them no harm. I had no love for Jacobites but this man was alone and he trusted them. I would not be part of this, so I pretended I had not heard.

'Captain,' I said, 'may I have the key to the whisky cupboard?'

'The weapons are in the same cupboard as the whisky!' whispered Riach.

'Aye!' said Hoseason. 'David can help. David's a good lad.' Turning back to me, he said, 'David, that wild Highlander is King George's enemy.'

They had never included me in the conversation before. I nodded innocently.

'We need the firearms from the roundhouse,' he said. 'He won't notice if you fetch out a pistol or two. I'll reward you well.'

I nodded, and went to the roundhouse. At the sight of the Jacobite prisoner calmly eating his supper, unaware of the danger, I knew I had to help him.

'You're in danger,' I said. 'The captain plans to murder you.'

He sprang to his feet. 'Will you stand with me?'

I said I would, and he asked my name. 'David Balfour,' I said, and, to impress him, added 'of the House of Shaws.'

'And I am Alan Breck Stewart,' he said proudly. 'Stewart is a king's name and needs nothing added to it.'

He examined the roundhouse for entry points. The skylight and the door were big enough to get through, so I went to shut the door.

'Leave it, David,' he said, 'so I can have my enemies in front of me. Excuse me calling you David, I forget the grand name of your estate. Load the pistols. How many in the crew?'

'Fifteen,' I said.

He let out a low whistle and raised his eyebrows. We were heavily outnumbered. 'I'll defend the door,' he said. 'Shoot if anyone passes the window, and keep reloading. Guard the skylight.'

'How, if I'm facing the window?' I said.

'Have you no ears in your head?' he asked.

'Oh, I see – I'll hear the glass break!' I said.

'You have a *bit* of sense, then,' replied Alan.

Suddenly, the captain appeared at the door. Alan drew his sword.

'This has sliced off more heads than you have toes on your feet!' he announced. 'Call your crew to fight!'

The captain looked past him at me. 'So you betrayed us,' he said. 'I won't forget it.'

He went away, and we stood ready. Alan held his sword in one hand and dirk[15] in the other. Outside, weapons clattered. There were fifteen men against Alan and me, and I had never even fired a pistol before. At least it would soon be over.

There was a roar, a rush, and a cry. Suddenly, Shuan was in the doorway with a sword, fighting Alan.

'Mind your window, David!' cried Alan as his sword pierced Shuan's body. Past the window ran five men with a battering ram. 'Take that!' I shouted, and fired. Someone screamed. My next two shots missed, but by then they were running away and sailors were dragging Shuan's body from the door. Alan's sword was reddened.

'They'll soon be back,' he said. 'In earnest, this time.'

The silence was more fearful than the fight. Presently, I heard quiet footsteps outside. Someone was on the roof – then a whistle blew, men rushed at the door, and the skylight shattered as a man leapt down. I clapped the pistol to his back, and could not bring myself to fire.

---

[15] A small dagger.

He whirled to face me. I know not whether it was fear or courage, but I fired and, as he fell, fired again at the man following him through the skylight.

Alan pulled his sword from the body of the man he had just killed and, with a roar, charged at the rest. They fled, and he chased them like a dog with sheep until they stumbled into the forecastle.

'What do you think of that?' he cried, and hugged me. 'I'm a bonny fighter!'

Four bodies lay on the floor, and he kicked them away. He was like a child with a new toy, whistling and boasting, but for me, the horror of what I had done was too great. I sat and sobbed. Alan put a hand on my shoulder to reassure me.

'You're a brave lad,' he said. 'You've done fine. You just need to sleep.'

We took turns to keep watch. By dawn, we were in sight of the Islands of the Hebrides.

The provisions were in the roundhouse, so I could have made a good breakfast – but the blood and broken glass all around us destroyed my appetite. Still, it was pleasant to think of Riach and Hoseason shut in the forecastle while the bottles were in the roundhouse.

'You did well last night,' said Alan. Taking a table knife, he carefully cut one of the fine silver buttons from his coat and handed it to me.

'These buttons belonged to my father,' he said. 'Wherever in the Highlands you show that button, the friends of Alan Breck will help you.' He said it as grandly as if he had an army at his command.

He was brushing his coat when Riach came to ask for a parley[16] and a dram.[17] The drink was given, and the

---

[16] A talk between two enemies, to arrange peace.

[17] A small drink of whisky.

captain came to the window.

'You've killed so many of my crew I can't work the ship,' he said. 'All I can do is to get you to Glasgow.'

'Where I can tell them all how a man and a boy saw you off?' said Alan. 'No, put me down in Appin, or thereabouts, but not in the Campbells' country.'

'It'll cost money,' said Hoseason.

'Sixty guineas to get me to Loch Linnhe,' said Alan.

The captain argued, but Alan had the upper hand. Two bottles of brandy were handed over, and the deal was settled.

CHAPTER 5

Shipwreck

Alan and I cleaned the roundhouse and exchanged our life stories. When I mentioned our minister, Mr Campbell, Alan cried out that he hated all Campbells.

'I would hunt them down,' he declared. 'I am a Stewart of Appin, and the Campbells have always cheated us with their lies and tricks! They're all on the side of the Whigs and the English! They won't stand and fight. They trick us with their lawyers and their dishonest ways of doing business.'

'Are you a good judge of business?' I asked, smiling.

Alan smiled, too. 'No, I'm as wasteful as my father, who taught me to use a sword,' he admitted. 'He was a valiant man, but never a rich one. He left me nothing but the clothes I wore. There was nothing for me to do but to enlist with the redcoats.'

'*What*?' I cried. 'You, in the English army?'

'A black spot on my character,' he admitted, 'but I deserted to the right side at the Battle of Prestonpans. If the redcoats catch me I'll be hanged for deserting, so now I live in France. I have a commission from the French King, so I'm a French officer now.'

'Why do you come back?' I asked.

'To serve Ardshiel, my clan chief,' he said. 'He and his family are in France, without the money that rightly belongs to him. His tenants in Appin, however poor they are, scrape a little rent together. His brother, James of the Glens, collects it, and I carry it to Ardshiel.'

Such loyalty impressed me. 'How noble of them!' I said.

'D'you think so? You're a Whig, but a gentleman,' he said. 'The Red Fox sees it differently.'

'The Red Fox?' I asked.

'Red-haired Colin Campbell of Glenure, he's the Red Fox,' he said fiercely. 'When the Highlanders were defeated and the English even forbade them to wear their own tartans, it wasn't enough for him. He wanted to destroy the clans. When he heard that the tenants were raising money for Ardshiel, he got permission from the government to turn them off their lands and out of their houses. May the Lord have mercy on him, if I ever find him!'

'You're a wanted man!' I said. 'How can you travel the Highlands safely?'

'You talk like a Whig,' he said. 'There are loyal friends there, and ways of hiding. The clans take care of each other, especially in these times, with so much to bear.

But how much *will* the Highlanders bear, I wonder? Sooner or later, some Highland laddie will put a bullet in the Red Fox.'

Late one night, Captain Hoseason came to the roundhouse and asked Alan if he could pilot the ship. Alan suspected a trick, but the captain was in earnest. He had never sailed round the Hebrides before, and had not known how dangerous these waters were. He feared he would lose the ship, for he had seen a dangerous reef[18] and was worried that there must be more. Alan and I went on deck.

'It's the Torran rocks,' said Alan. 'There's ten miles of them.'

Whatever Hoseason and Riach were guilty of, they were expert sailors and determined to save the ship. They had almost brought her safely through the rocks when a sudden surge of the tide caught us and flung the ship round. We struck against the reef with a crash that threw us off our feet. Breakers hurled against us, grinding the brig[19] upon the rocks.

---

[18] A row of rocks close to the surface of the water.
[19] A ship with two masts and large square sails.

Riach, the sailors, and I struggled through the waves to release the ship's small boat, the skiff.[20] It was no easy task, with the sea breaking over us and the skiff fastened amidships,[21] but we freed it at last. Someone shouted, 'Hold on!'

The next wave was so huge it lifted the ship and turned her right over. I sank, surfaced and sank again, hurled and choked by the sea. Grabbing a piece of driftwood, I clung to it and looked round.

I had been swept into quiet waters. I could hardly swim at all, but ahead, I could see a small island. Kicking

[20] A small boat kept on a ship.
[21] The middle of a ship.

46

and hanging onto the driftwood, I struggled to a sandy bay. It was bare and deserted, but at least it was land.

I spent a miserable night alone, chilled, soaked, and in darkness. As soon as there was daylight, I climbed a hill. There was no sign of the ship, nor of anything else. The land was deserted, and I was desperately hungry.

I explored my tiny islet. All that separated it from the next larger island was a small inlet, or creek. From what I had heard from Alan and the crew, I worked out that the larger island must be the Isle of Mull, and there were people living there. If only I could get to Mull I could find help, and cross to the mainland.

I tried to cross the inlet but it was too deep to wade and too far to swim, so I searched for the driftwood that had saved my life. To my dismay, I saw it floating out to sea, and I confess I wept with despair at the sight. I was stranded, with no food and no chance of escape.

I ate raw shellfish, but they made me violently ill. Rain fell all day, and at night I sheltered as well as I could between two rocks. In the morning I found a hill from which I could see the islands of Iona and Mull, and they gave me a faint hope. I could see houses, and perhaps I could hail a boat.

Too late, I found a hole in my pocket. Now who would help me? Of all the money I had, I was left with only three guineas and four shillings in the world. I was not only homeless – I would be wretchedly poor if I ever reached the outside world again. My clothes began to rot because of the salt water. Each day I grew weaker and more ill, and my throat burned.

At last, there was a day of sunshine and I sat on the hill to dry myself and my clothes. To my joy, I saw a boat. I leapt up, waving and shouting, knowing that the boatmen saw me. They pointed at me, called out something in Gaelic, and laughed – but they did not stop. They sailed on past me, and out of sight.

It was more grief than I knew how to bear. I raged, and, I admit, wept, like a furious child. Such wretchedness was too much for me.

When, next day, I saw the boat again, I dared not hope. This time, she headed towards the island. I stumbled to the shore to meet the crew but they spoke quickly in Gaelic, which I did not understand. The skipper attempted English, waved his arms, and pointed, and I caught the word, 'tide'.

I learned at last what he was trying to tell me. It was only an island at high tide! The channel that had been too deep and wide to cross became dry whenever the tide was out. They had wondered why I had stayed on the island when I could have walked to Mull on any day since I arrived, and, at last, they had come to explain it to me.

If only I had thought harder instead of raging, I would have worked it out for myself. It should have been obvious to a fool.

CHAPTER 6

The Silver Button

When the tide was out I walked across to Mull and came at last to a low, stone house with a turf roof. The old man I found there spoke a little English, and I asked him if he had seen any of my shipmates.

'Ah!' he said. 'The lad with the silver button!'

'Why yes!' I said.

'Your friend told me,' he said, 'that you are to follow him to Appin, which is his own country, by way of Torosay.'

Then with great kindness and pleasant manners he took me into the house, where his wife gave me the first good food and drink I had tasted for days. I slept that night in the smoky house, and, next day, made my way across Mull. I still wanted to face my uncle and claim my inheritance, but first it seemed sensible to find Alan. In these unfamiliar Highlands, he was the only friend I had.

In those days, soon after the 1745 Rebellion, there was great poverty in the Highlands and islands. Even in a place as remote as Mull, I met beggars. The wearing of tartans and kilts was forbidden, and the islanders wore all manner of strange outfits as they tried to keep as much of their traditional wear as possible.

Over the next two days, two different guides offered to take me to Torosay. One turned out to be a heavy drinker and the other was a blind man who claimed to be a preacher.

Both tried to cheat me of my remaining money, but I came at last to Torosay and from there I could see Morven, on the mainland. In four days I had walked the fifty miles from one end of Mull to the other.

I took the ferry from Torosay to the mainland. The ferryman was named Neil Roy Macrob, and knowing that the Macrobs were kin to Alan, I hoped for news of him. There I made a mistake, for I mentioned Alan and

offered Neil Roy a shilling. He was deeply offended, so I tried showing him the silver button instead.

'Why did you not say you were the lad with the silver button, instead of insulting a Highland gentleman with your dirty money!' he said. 'You are to make your way to Ardgour and stay at the house of John of the Claymore, who is expecting you. Then cross the two lochs at Corran and Balachulish and ask your way to the house of James of the Glens, at Aucharn. Keep well away from Whigs, Campbells, and redcoats.'

The following day I met and travelled with a preacher, Mr Henderland, who knew of Alan. I was eager for any news he could give me.

'Who knows where Alan Breck Stewart might be?' he said. 'He's here and away like a heathercat![22] But everyone knows where Colin Campbell is.'

'The Red Fox?' I said.

'Aye,' said Henderland. 'He's in Appin, turning Highlanders out of their homes under the very nose of Ardshiel's brother, James of the Glens. When he's finished there, he'll do the same thing in Cameron country. It's my belief that if the Stewarts don't kill him, the Camerons will.'

---

[22] A fierce Scottish wildcat.

CHAPTER 7

Murder

In the morning I crossed Loch Linnhe on a fishing boat. From the loch I saw bare mountains and little watercourses, and something bright that glinted in the sun.

'What's that?' I asked the boatman.

'The sun on the soldiers' weapons,' he said. 'They are evicting the tenants at Appin.'

When we entered Loch Leven I asked to be set down on the shores, for I knew that we were in Appin, Alan's home country. They left me by a wood at a place called Lettermore, and I sat in a birch wood to eat some oat bread Mr Henderland had given me. I was trying to make up my mind whether to continue looking for Alan or simply go south and find Mr Rankeillor, when I heard voices, horses' hooves, and jingling harnesses.

Four travellers were approaching. One was a large red-haired man who sweated in the heat. The others, judging by their clothes, were a lawyer, a servant, and an officer of the law. I jumped up and asked them the way to Aucharn, in Appin.

'What do you want in Aucharn?' said the red-haired

man.

'Someone who lives there,' I said.

'Be careful, Glenure,' said the lawyer. Glenure! I recognized that name. The red-haired man was Colin Campbell of Glenure, the Red Fox!

'Someone who lives there? You mean James, the brother of Ardshiel?' demanded the Red Fox. 'Why do you seek him?'

He turned to the lawyer, but before either of them could speak there was a gunshot. With a cry of pain, Colin Campbell fell to the ground.

The lawyer caught him in his arms. Helpless and horrified I watched as, with fear in his eyes, Colin Campbell gave a great sigh and lay dead.

I swung round in the direction of the shot. A big man with a gun moved through the heather. 'The murderer!' I cried, and scrambled up the hillside. From all directions redcoats were running to the wood, and the lawyer shouted to them.

'Catch that lad!' he cried. 'He is an accomplice. He was sent to keep us talking.'

It had never occurred to me that anyone would think me guilty. Amazed and helpless, I ran, with the soldiers pursuing me.

'Come in here!' said a voice, among the trees.

I obeyed, ducking into the cover as gunshots flew

around me.

There, hiding among the trees was Alan, holding a fishing rod. 'Come!' he said. I followed him, weaving and crawling through the heather. From time to time Alan would stand upright and look over his shoulder, so that all the soldiers saw him and roared. Just when my heart was ready to burst with the effort, Alan threw himself down in the heather.

'Now it's in earnest,' he said. 'Do as I do.' This time, crawling with our faces to the heather and taking great care not to be seen, we crept back to the place where I had first found Alan. There, deep in the wood of Lettermore, we lay on the bracken, exhausted.

The horror of my situation came home to me. I had seen Colin Campbell murdered and, because I had kept them talking in the road, I was suspected of assisting the murderer. Now I was with Alan, who hated Campbell and wanted him dead. Had Alan killed him in cold blood?

'I must part from you, Alan,' I said, when I caught my breath. 'We cannot stay together after this.'

'For what reason?' asked Alan. 'Is this some insult against my honour?'

'Alan, that man lies dead,' I said.

Alan said nothing for a while, then, 'Mr Balfour, if I were going to kill a gentleman I would not do it in my own country, where it would bring trouble on my clan. And I would take a sword and a gun, not a fishing rod. I swear to you by all that is holy, I had no part in it.'

'Thank God!' I cried. 'Do you know who did it?'

'He passed close by me,' said Alan innocently, 'but I was tying my shoes, and did not get a good look at him.'

'Alan,' I said, 'can you swear you don't know him?'

'Not yet,' he admitted, 'but give me time. I'm awful good at forgetting.'

'You were letting the soldiers see you!' I cried. 'You did that to draw them away from the murderer!'

'Well, he would have done the same for me,' he said. 'We should get away now. We must not be caught, David. I am a deserter, and they think you are an accomplice in the murder.'

'But if I'm caught, I'll get a fair trial,' I said.

'Oh, David!' he cried. 'Have you no idea of the Highlands? The law here is in the hands of the Campbells! Of course you'd get no fair trial!'

The idea of running and hiding through the heather did not appeal to me, but the thought of being hanged for murder was far worse. If I had to flee I could eventually go south, and confront my uncle.

'I'll go with you,' I said.

As we set out for Aucharn, Alan told me what happened after the shipwreck. When the *Covenant* finally went down and they had swum to the shore, Hoseason called on the crew to murder Alan for his money. Riach alone had come to Alan's defence, and the crew had ended up fighting among themselves on the beach.

'The little man, Riach, cried to me to run,' he said. 'It struck me as a wise remark. So I ran.'

It was night by the time we reached the house of James of the Glens, high in steep mountains. People were hurrying in and out with lighted torches. A tall, handsome man in middle age came to the gate. Alan greeted him, and introduced me to James of the Glens.

'This is a dreadful day for us all,' complained James.

'Be thankful Colin Campbell is dead!' said Alan.

'Aye, but the people of Appin will suffer for it,' said James, twisting his hands together. 'I have all the clan and my own family to think of. We are burying our weapons in the moss, for we will be searched.'

All this time, anxious servants were scurrying about with bundles. James led us into the house, where his wife and son sat by the fire, burning sheaf after sheaf of papers. His wife wiped tears from her face as James paced about restlessly. His anxiety made him bad-tempered with his family, which, as a stranger, I would rather not have watched.

Alan and I were given a change of clothes, and Alan told James our story. Everyone agreed that we should flee, and the servants began at once to pack for our

journey. They bundled up oatmeal, a pan, swords and pistols, and brandy. The gold in Alan's money belt had been sent by another messenger to Ardshiel in France by this time, so we had only our own money left. There was very little. James gave what he could, but it made small difference.

'Get away quickly,' said James. 'Alan, if you and your friend are arrested for the murder, I will be suspected too. I am your kinsman, so they will think I'm involved. You and I have always been good friends, but if I am blamed, I must paper both of you.'

'Paper?' I asked.

'Put a paper out against us,' said Alan. 'A handbill,[23] accusing us of the murder and offering a reward.' He pointed out that this was hard on me, but James could only think of the danger to himself and his family.

'I don't understand this at all,' I said. 'Why don't you paper the real murderer?'

Alan and James were horrified. 'But he might be caught!' exclaimed James. 'What would the Camerons think of us if we did that?'

This convinced me of two things. Firstly, that the murderer was a Cameron and secondly, that there was no point in arguing. The fact that they were putting me in danger to protect him was, to them, necessary. It was

---

[23] A poster.

part of their Highland idea of honour, and I had to accept it.

'Well, paper who you like,' I said. James's wife leapt from her chair, hugged me and thanked me. Then, Alan and I left, to travel south by night under cover of darkness.

Alan had to get to France, and I aimed to get back to Queensferry and find Mr Rankeillor, the family lawyer. But for now, the important thing was to get well away from Aucharn.

CHAPTER 8

On the Run

A night of walking and running brought us to the rocky valley of Glencoe. It was a bare place, offering little shelter, and Alan was sure the redcoats would watch it. The sooner we could cross it, the better.

We ran harder than ever, leaping over wide rivers and across rocks so high they made me dizzy. I tried not to look down at the waterfalls, for it made my head spin. Alan found it easy and I did my best to keep up, but we came to a high rock made slippery with spray. The waterfall roared beneath us, and the leap was wider than any I had ever done. With the rush of water sounding in my ears, I could not move.

'Hang or drown!' yelled Alan. He leapt, and knowing I had no choice, I followed him. I fell, tried to grab the slippery rock, and was pulled to safety by Alan's waiting hands. Then he turned and went on running as I stumbled after him. He led us to rocks so steep even he had difficulty climbing them, but at last we dragged ourselves to the top. To me, the high rocks seemed a good place to hide.

'You're not so good at jumping,' he said, 'but you

made a good try.'

I fell asleep on the rocks at last, but was woken by Alan whispering.

I looked down. Redcoats were all over the valley.

'What can we do?' I whispered.

'Stay here and be cooked,' he said.

It was already hot, and grew hotter as the sun rose higher. Hour after hour, the sun struck down, the rock heated like a griddle, and we had no water. We lay helpless and parched, baking on that rock. The soldiers came so near, we hardly dared breathe.

Far into the afternoon a shadow fell on one side of our rock and we lay in its shelter, sweating and aching. When the soldiers took a rest and were falling asleep, we knew we must take the risk of slipping through the valley. It was so silent that a falling pebble would have alerted them.

As the sun was setting we came to a deep rushing burn[24] and with joy we hurled ourselves into the water, splashing and drinking. Then we made a little porridge of oatmeal and water, and, refreshed, walked on through the night.

Alan led the way to a cleft in the mountaintop, called the Heugh of Corrynakiegh. It was wooded with pine and birch trees, and there was a cave where we could shelter. We slept on heather and ate trout, which we caught with our hands in the burn. For five days we sheltered there,

---

[24] A stream.

while Alan taught me to use a sword. We could not stay in one place for long, though, and Alan said we would need more money for the rest of our journey.

'We must send a message to James of the Glens, to ask for money,' he said. 'David, may I borrow the silver button? I don't wish to cut another.'

I gave him the button and he made a little cross out of wood. He tied the silver button into it, with some sprigs of birch and fir.

'I have a cousin living nearby,' he said. 'We must not risk being seen, but if I leave this in his window he will understand it. He will see the cross, which is a sign of a meeting. He will know who that button belongs to, and will know that he is to meet Alan Breck. The birch and fir will tell him that he is to meet me in a place of birches and firs. There are not many such places nearby, so he will know where to come.'

'Wouldn't it be easier to write him a letter?' I asked.

'Aye,' teased Alan, 'but he'd have to go to school for a year or two and learn to read, and we might be wearied waiting!'

The signal worked. His cousin found the cross and came to the wood, but he was terrified of helping us. He sullenly agreed to take a message to James, and set off.

He returned after three days with a note from James's wife. James had been arrested as an accomplice in the murder. She sent the little money she could scrape together for us, and a handbill with a description of Alan and myself. We were both wanted for the murder of the Red Fox.

We read our descriptions with interest. Alan was 'a small, pock-marked man, about thirty-five, in a French coat with tarnished lace, and silver buttons'. Alan was most indignant about the lace. I was 'a tall lad of about eighteen in an old blue coat, blue breeches, and a homespun[25] waistcoat.'

Fortunately, I was no longer wearing those clothes, but Alan was very proud of his coat. I told him it made him conspicuous, but he would not seek a different one.

This meant that Alan, because of his vanity, was more in danger of arrest than I was. Besides, he intended to go to France. I only wanted to reach Queensferry to find Mr Rankeillor, the lawyer. Alan's journey would cost far more than mine. I began to think I would be better off without him.

Eleven hours walking led us to a vast stretch of moorland. It was an exposed place, but we had no choice other than to cross it. We saw no soldiers, but there were mountains all round. If the redcoats came over those mountains, they were sure to see us.

It was a long wearying landscape of heather, peat, and dead trees. Large stretches of heather had been burned in a heath fire, and smelt sharp and bitter. We tried to find

---

[25] Plain, simple material.

hollow places to creep through, crawling from one bush to another like hunters.

For hour after hour, in blistering sunshine, we went on. The water-bottle was empty, and the constant stooping and crawling made my limbs ache. At about noon we rested in a thick patch of heather to take turns sleeping and keeping watch.

Alan took first watch, but when he wakened me I was still heavily drowsy. In the hot, heathery smell and the drone of bees, I struggled to stay awake.

With a sudden jerk I woke, and realized I had fallen asleep on watch. Soldiers were riding their horses through the heather.

I woke Alan. He glanced at the soldiers, then at the sun, but he said not a word to blame me. He pointed to a mountain far away.

'That's Ben [26] Alder,' he said. 'We'll be safe there.'

'We'll have to cross the soldiers' path!' I said, but there was nothing else we could do. Alan ran forwards on hands and knees at an amazing speed, weaving his way through the heather. The pace was hard, the dust and reek of burnt moor stung my throat, my wrists and knees ached, and still we could not stop.

It grew harder. Even Alan was breathless. The dust in my eyes almost blinded me, the pain in my joints was

---

[26] Mountain – the names of most Scottish mountains begin with 'Ben'.

excruciating. At twilight we saw the soldiers making camp for the night, and I begged Alan to stop.

'We must reach Ben Alder by night,' he said.

'I cannot!' I said.

'Then I'll carry you,' said Alan. He was a small man, but he meant it, and I felt ashamed.

'I'll keep going,' I said.

The night was cooler and dew fell, but in my heart I

was raging. I had to crawl in pain like a hunted beast. As long as Alan led, I must follow, and I hated him for it. I felt I had been crawling in agony all my life. Sleepless and wretched, we ran straight into an ambush. A few ragged men leapt from the heath, and seized us.

I no longer cared if they killed me. Alan spoke to one of our captors, then he turned to me, smiling.

'This is good!' he said. 'They are Cluny Macpherson's men. They'll take us to him.'

I had heard of Cluny Macpherson, a clan chief who was outlawed after the 1745 Rebellion. Alan was delighted at the prospect of being his guest, but I cared about nothing. My head was light and spinning, I felt sickened, and could not walk or speak. Two of Cluny's men half-carried me to their stronghold.

CHAPTER 9

Cluny's Cage

'Cluny's Cage' was built into the cliff side from tree
trunks, dried mud, and moss. As Cluny was an outlaw, it
was only one of his hideouts.

Cluny himself came out to meet us. He was plainly
dressed and smoked a foul-smelling pipe, but he
welcomed us with the manners of a king.

'Welcome, Mr Stewart, sir, and to your friend,' he said warmly. Alan introduced me grandly as 'the Laird[27] of House of Shaws, Mr David Balfour.' Whenever Alan introduced me to his friends, he stopped sneering at my title and boasted about it.

I found that Cluny, outlaw though he was, ruled from his cage like a king with trusted servants to attend him. Clansmen came to him to settle any disputes between them. He graciously served us food he had prepared himself, but I was too ill to take anything but a drink.

When the meal was over, Cluny brought out an old greasy pack of cards. With a twinkle in his eyes, he invited us to play.

I was deeply shocked, for my father had always taught me that gambling was wicked and disgraceful. I told Cluny that I objected to cards, and would not play.

'This is Whig talk,' cried Cluny, 'in my own house!'

'Mr Balfour is an honest gentleman and my good friend,' said Alan. 'But he's tired. I'm willing to play.'

'I am keeping a promise to my father,' I said. Still annoyed, but accepting my decision, Cluny pointed me to a bed of heather. I lay down and gave in to the fever that was taking hold of me.

For two days I was confused and delirious, sometimes awake and sometimes not. When I woke, I was aware of

---

[27] A Scottish landowner.

Alan and Cluny playing cards with heaps of gold on the table. At one point, Alan leaned over and asked to borrow my money. I was too ill to refuse.

On the third day I felt better, but I was still very weak. Cluny had heard that there were no soldiers about in the south, so it would be a good chance for us to get away, but it worried me that Alan looked uneasy and avoided my gaze.

'The little money we have won't take us far,' I said.

'I've lost it,' muttered Alan. 'My money, and yours. All of it. I have no sense when I get to the cards.'

'It's only a game!' said Cluny. 'Take your money back again, and welcome. Take double!' He pulled gold from his pocket. 'I will not take advantage of you.'

Alan only looked at the ground. I asked Cluny for a word in private.

'It's lonely up here,' he said. 'It's pleasant to have a friend to play cards with. If my friends lose . . .'

'You give them back their money,' I said. 'And if they win, they carry off your money. Can't you see it insults my pride to accept?'

'I do not invite guests to insult them,' he said stiffly. 'Take the money. You're as welcome to it as if you were my own son. Shake hands on it!'

I did as he said, but the hurt to my pride was deep, and I could not ignore it. Alan's behaviour had left me humiliated.

Cluny's gillies[28] left us at Loch Rannoch, and we walked on in resentful silence. I was still angry at Alan's foolishness with the cards. I knew he was ashamed, and angry at me because I took it so badly – but I had good reason to!

---

[28] Chief's attendants, traditionally in charge of hunting.

The more we trudged on, the more I wanted to part from him, even though I knew that, in everything but the cards, he had been a good friend. The thought of leaving him shamed me, so I tried to tell myself it would be a noble act. He would be safer alone.

Because I could not speak pleasantly to him, I did not speak at all. At last, Alan broke the silence.

'This is no way for friends to behave,' he said. 'I'm sorry for what happened. Have you anything to say?'

'Nothing,' I said, which did not help.

'I admit, I was to blame,' he said.

'Yes, you were,' I said, 'but I had not mentioned it.'

'You have made mistakes yourself.' Alan was growing irritated. 'If you want us to part, there's enough room in Scotland. We need never see each other again.'

This hurt. It was as if he knew my disloyal thoughts.

'Alan!' I cried. 'I will not desert you! Haven't I stayed loyal to you? Do you blame me for falling asleep on the moor? There are things between us that I can't forget, even if you can!'

'You mean that I owe you my life,' he said. 'You need not make it a burden for me.'

By this time I was angry with myself, too, for I knew I was being unreasonable. I turned that anger on Alan.

'You admit that you were at fault,' I said. 'Am I supposed to thank you?'

We fell back into silence. For three days, we hardly spoke. My fever was returning, but I refused Alan's offers of help until I had exhausted his patience and he no longer attempted to be kind. Instead he would walk jauntily ahead, whistling and giving an irritating smile.

In the continuous rain and wind, my sickness grew worse. My teeth chattered, my throat burned, and a pain in my side gripped me.

Alan taunted me all the time. 'Whig' was all he ever called me. If I struggled to jump over a stream, he laughed and teased me. As I grew worse, I believed that I would soon die, and like a sullen schoolboy I comforted myself with the thought that, then, Alan would be sorry.

At last, with my legs buckling under me and the pain in my side unbearable, I could not go on. Alan had just called me 'Whig' again.

'Have you no manners, Mr Stewart?' I said. He stood with a sneer on his face, and whistled a Jacobite tune.

'Be civil to King George,' I said. 'You fought for him once. Now, you run for your life from his soldiers. Aye, and the Campbells too. Yes, I know you bear a king's name. So do many of your friends, and they'd be none the worse for washing.'

'You insult me,' said Alan. 'I cannot forgive such insults.'

'I don't ask you to,' I said, and drew my sword. 'I am ready.'

'Are you mad, Davie?' he cried. 'It would be murder!'

'That was your look-out when you insulted me,' I said, standing on guard.

He drew his sword, but before I could move he had

thrown it to the ground. 'I cannot!' he cried. 'I cannot hurt you!'

My anger drained away from me. I remembered all his kindness and courage in the past – then the pain in my side overcame me. An apology would not have moved him, but a cry for help brought Alan to my side.

'I'm finished,' I said. 'I shall die here. I can hardly breathe for pain. Can you forgive me?'

'Wheesht!' He put an arm round me to help me along. 'We'll find a house. If you can't walk, I'll carry you.'

'I'm too heavy for you!' I said. 'Why do you care for me, when I'm so ungrateful?'

'I've no idea!' he said. 'I liked you because you never quarrelled – and now, I like you better!'

CHAPTER 10

Mr Rankeillor

Alan got us to a house in Balquhidder where a Maclaren family, loyal to the Stewarts, welcomed us in. They had heard of Alan, and admired him. A handbill giving our description and offering a reward for us had been published – there was a copy pinned to the foot of my bed! I think most of Balquhidder knew we were there, but nobody betrayed us. A doctor was sent for, and we stayed until I was well.

Alan could not stay anywhere long without finding a quarrel. One night the house was visited by Robin Oig, the son of the famous Rob Roy Macgregor, and the Macgregors and Stewarts were old enemies. Alan and Robin eyed each other like fighting dogs, traded insults and nearly came to blows, but Mr Maclaren was a wise man. He pointed out that they were both fine pipers, and offered his pipes so we could tell who played the best.

Both Robin's playing and Alan's were breathtaking, but at last, Robin played a lament.[29] Alan had no thought for anything but the music.

'Robin Oig,' he said, 'I am not fit to make music in the

---

[29] A sad tune, usually mourning for a death.

same kingdom as you.' All quarrels were forgotten, and there was music, talk, and drinking long into the night.

It was late August, we were short of money, and I urgently needed to reach Mr Rankeillor. The hunt for us had slackened and Alan was sure we would be safe when we had crossed the river Forth. We meant to cross at

Stirling Bridge, but it was heavily guarded. We had no choice but to go to the Firth of Forth, and hire a boat.

'How can we pay for a boat?' I said.

'I'll think of something,' said Alan. 'Beg, borrow, steal, or make one. Leave it to Alan!'

Tired and hungry, we reached Limekilns, and found ourselves amongst farms, villages, and green hills again. At an inn we bought bread and cheese and we sat on the shore to eat it, looking across to Queensferry.

'You remember the lass who sold us the bread?' asked Alan.

'She was a nice-looking lass,' I replied.

'I'm glad you think so,' said Alan. 'It could help us to get a boat.'

'It would be more useful if she thought the same about me,' I said.

'That's not the point. I don't want her to fall in love with you,' said Alan. 'I want her to feel sorry for you, and get us a boat. You look pale and tatty enough. We'll do a bit of play-acting.'

He made me hang on his arm as he walked back into the inn, calling for brandy. This he gave to me in little sips, looking anxiously at my face.

'Is he not well?' asked the girl.

'Not well? He's walked hundreds of miles and slept every night in wet heather!' cried Alan.

'Is there nobody to help him?' she said.

'Aye, if we could reach them,' said Alan, and he whistled a Jacobite tune. With a few whispers and suggestions he convinced her that I was a young Jacobite laird who would be hanged if I could not be smuggled to the protection of my friends. She brought us ale and hot food, and Alan convinced her that what we needed most was a boat.

'If I can get him to Mr Rankeillor,' he said, 'he will be safe.'

The name of Mr Rankeillor was enough. She herself brought us a boat that night, borrowed without permission from a neighbour, and rowed us across the Forth. I was left with something new to feel guilty about, for I wished we had not involved her in our dangers.

We agreed that Alan should lie low next day. He would stay in the fields near the road while I went to Queensferry, and I would whistle a Highland tune as a signal when it was safe for him to come out.

By sunrise I was in Queensferry, where the smart town streets made me ashamed of the rags I had worn for so long. I only hoped I could convince Mr Rankeillor that I really was David Balfour, and that my story was true. I had no idea where his house was, and, shabby as I was, I felt too ashamed to ask anyone. After a morning spent wandering round the town I stopped outside a large, elegant house when a well-dressed man came out, noticed me, and came to speak to me. He had a kind face and a helpful manner, and I told him I needed to find Mr Rankeillor.

'Remarkable!' he said. 'I *am* Mr Rankeillor! May I know your name?'

'David Balfour,' I said. He looked greatly surprised and I am sure he did not believe me, but he invited me into the house.

He asked first about my parents and my place of birth, to satisfy himself that I was who I claimed to be. Then I told him of my kidnap, and the loss of the ship.

'The *Covenant*,' he said, 'sailed on the 27th June, and it is now the 24th August. I wonder where you have been since. Mr Campbell, the minister of Essendean, has been here to ask about you. He had heard no news of you, and was worried. Your uncle Ebenezer said that he had given you money and you had gone away to begin a new life in Europe. Then Captain Hoseason arrived in my office, insisting that you had been on the *Covenant* and drowned. He must have hoped to be paid for the information. Now, exactly what have you been doing these last two months?'

'To tell you that,' I said, 'I must trust you with the life of my friend. He is an innocent man, wrongly wanted for murder.' Then I told him all my story. When I mentioned Alan Breck Stewart, he looked up sharply.

'If the man wanted for the Appin murder is close by, I don't want to know it,' he said. 'Shall we call Alan "Mr Thomson" so no one will know we mean him?' Then he let me go on with my story.

'Well, you and your friend seem to have rolled all over Scotland,' he said, 'but I think your troubles are over.'

He called a servant to set another place at the table because I was to stay for dinner. Then he provided me with water, soap, a comb, and clean clothes, and left me to become myself again. When I had washed and changed, he took me to his study and told me something I had never known about my own family.

'Let me explain,' Mr Rankeillor said, 'about your father and your uncle, Alexander and Ebenezer. Alexander was the elder brother and a kind young man, but quiet and unsure of himself. Ebenezer was the handsome, adventurous one who rode about the country impressing the ladies.'

'Uncle Ebenezer?' I said in disbelief.

'In those days he was a spirited young man, and a spoiled one, too. He and your father both fell in love with the same lady. Ebenezer was used to getting his own way in everything. There was a great deal of arguing about it. Ebenezer screamed, made himself ill, and poured out his miseries to anyone who would listen. Your father took far too much notice of him. At one point, the lady turned them both away.

Eventually, your father offered to give up his claim to the House of Shaws if Ebenezer would not pursue the lady. Ebenezer agreed. Your father gave up his inheritance, married the lady, went to Essendean and became a poor schoolmaster. Ebenezer had the house and land and all that went with it, but he knew he had won it unfairly. So did his neighbours, who despised him. Some even thought he must have murdered your father. He had exchanged love for money, and money became all he cared for. It made a harsh landlord of him. Over the years he became what he is today – selfish, suspicious, and old before his time.'

'Then does the House of Shaws rightly belong to him, or to me?' I asked.

'Oh, to you,' said Mr Rankeillor. 'The arrangement between the brothers was not legally binding. The House of Shaws is yours. But if you claim it, Ebenezer will fight you for it. We have to prove that your story is true and that you really are David Balfour, and that would mean an expensive lawsuit. We would have to ask your friend, "Mr Thomson", to give evidence, and that is something we should avoid. No, I think we should come to some arrangement with your uncle. If we can prove that he arranged to have you kidnapped, he will be too frightened to argue with us.'

This gave me an idea. I explained it to Mr Rankeillor and we decided to put my plan into action. Mr Rankeillor sent for his clerk, Mr Torrance, for we would need his help, and after we had eaten we set off to find Alan – or 'Mr Thomson', as we called him. He, too, was part of our plan. Mr Torrance carried a covered basket and a legal document, which Mr Rankeillor had just drawn up. I went ahead, whistling the Highland air I shall remember for the rest of my life.

Alan was delighted to hear of the plan and of his part in it. We set out for the House of Shaws, and arrived there that night. While I hid in the shadows with Mr Rankeillor and Mr Torrance, Alan strode up to the door and began to knock.

———◆◆◆———

In My Kingdom

There was a long wait, while Alan banged at the door.

Eventually my uncle opened an upstairs window and snarled, 'Who are you, and what do you want?'

'It is not my business I come upon,' said Alan calmly. 'It's yours. It's about David Balfour, your nephew.'

My uncle's manner changed abruptly. 'I'd better let you in,' he muttered.

'Do I *want* to come in?' said Alan. 'I am just as proud as you are and of better family, and I prefer to talk on the doorstep.'

Uncle Ebenezer muttered to himself and presently we heard him scraping back the bolts and chains on the door. He appeared with the blunderbuss and sat on the doorstep pointing the gun at Alan, who was not at all impressed by it.

'Your young nephew, David Balfour,' he said, 'was shipwrecked off the Isle of Mull and fell into the hands of friends of mine. They are rough, wild gentlemen and have no wish to keep him eating at their expense. I think, for the payment of a reasonable sum of money, they will return him to you.'

'You mean they want ransom money?' said Ebenezer.
'I'm paying nothing. I don't want him back.'

'Then I expect they'll let him go,' said Alan, 'and he
can wander where he wants. Back here, possibly. Is that
what you want? He may have things to tell about you,
Mr Balfour, that you would rather keep quiet. What do

you want us to do with him?'

My uncle shuffled about and made no answer.

'Come, do you answer or do I run a sword through you?' demanded Alan. 'In plain speaking, do you want my friends to kill David Balfour, or keep him? Killed or kept?'

My uncle moaned and grumbled. At last, he said, 'Oh, kept! He's my brother's son!'

I remembered that this had not stopped him from trying to kill me before. Perhaps that occasion had frightened him so much that he dared not try it again.

'Then we must agree a price for his keep,' said Alan. 'That's a hard thing to decide. What did you pay Hoseason to kidnap him?'

'How do you know that?' demanded my uncle. 'It wasn't a kidnap. I just paid him twenty pounds to take the lad and sell him in Carolina.'

Mr Rankeillor stepped from the shadows. 'Thank you,' he said. 'That is all we needed.'

'And I am a witness,' said Mr Torrance.

'Good evening, uncle,' I said.

My uncle stood like a man turned to stone. He did not resist as Alan took the blunderbuss from him, led him indoors, and sat him down. Mr Torrance brought wine from the cellar, and Mr Rankeillor presented my uncle with the document he had written out earlier. Uncle

Ebenezer, having just confessed to the kidnap in front of witnesses, could hardly argue. I pitied his shame.

The agreement put Mr Rankeillor in charge of our affairs, and I was to have two-thirds of the income of the House of Shaws. We celebrated the arrangement with a good supper from the basket Mr Torrance carried, and at last I lay down in the kitchen to sleep.

I had a home, and my life before me. In spite of Uncle Ebenezer's miserable way of living, there was still enough money and land to give me a good income. I really was David Balfour of the House of Shaws.

In our months of escaping through the heather I had learned to sleep in cold and wet, however hungry I was. Now, warm and well fed, I lay awake. I watched the patterns of firelight on the ceiling, and imagined my future.

I needed Mr Rankeillor's advice on other matters, and most of all on how to get Alan to France. Mr Rankeillor set about finding a ship and arranging to get him safely aboard. There was another, harder problem, too. James of the Glens was still in prison, awaiting trial as an accomplice in the murder of the Red Fox, and I wanted to help him.

'If you give evidence for James,' said Mr Rankeillor,

'you will end up in the dock beside him, wrongly charged with being an accomplice to murder. You could be condemned to death.'

'Then I'd just have to be hanged, wouldn't I?' I said.

'My dear boy!' he cried. 'If you think you must take the risk, then do. Better than living safe and ashamed.'

He gave me a letter to the British Linen Company, which was a bank. They would give me access to my own money so I could afford a lawyer who would defend me, and he recommended a man in whom he had absolute confidence. If I wanted to help James, the British Linen Company Bank was the place to start, but first, I must part from Alan.

I went with him as far as the pass at the place called Rest and Be Thankful. We talked of our plans to keep in touch, and of the times we had spent together, but our speech was awkward and uneasy because we knew this was the end of our road together. We parted with strong feelings but few words and one final handshake. Walking back to the city alone, I felt so abandoned that I wanted to sit down and weep like a child.

In the afternoon I passed into Edinburgh, not thinking of where I was going. I thought of Alan and wished I could have been of more help to him, although I knew he was going to be safe. But, at last, as I wandered through the streets, I found myself standing at the door

of the British Linen Company Bank, and I knew what I must do next.

So this is the end of the story of my kidnap and my return to my inheritance. All went well with Alan and me, and whatever came to us, it was not dishonour.